Serendipity & Me

Serendipity & Me

BY

JUDITH L. ROTH

SCHOLASTIC INC.

ISBN 978-0-545-62621-7

12 11 10 9 8 7 6 5 4 3 2   14 15 16 17 18/0

Printed in the U.S.A.   40

First Scholastic printing, September 2013

Set in Excelsior

Book design by Nancy Brennan

The three poems quoted in *Serendipity and Me*, "The Look," "I Shall Not Care," and a selection from "A November Night," come from the collection *Love Songs*, by Sara Teasdale (New York: The Macmillan Company, 1917).

✿

FOR MARC, in gratitude and love—from that first
dorm kitty to children, grown, our life together
has been a blessing. . . .

✿

ser•en•dip•i•ty (ser-ən-'*di*-pə-tē) n. 1. The ability to
make lucky discoveries. 2. A happy surprise.

kit•ty ('*ki*-tē) n. What you call a cat when you like it.

✿

I remember
my mom quoting
"The fog comes
on little cat feet"
And my dad replying
"More like big elephant feet"

because the fog here
in Central California
is a dense gray wall
that bellows in its silence

Tule

sounds like *toolie*
named for grass
growing in wetlands
where this fog forms

Tule

sounds like *boonies*
like out in the boonies

where this fog is thickest

like out in the Tule boonies
where my mom
was lost to me

forever

It starts as a tickle
        in the back of my throat.

But I can't pay attention
        because Mrs. Detweiler
        (the other sixth-grade teacher, not mine)
        is going over prerehearsal notes,
        is saying, *Channel your mother, Sara,*
        thinking she's being cute
        because you only channel someone
        who's dead.

She doesn't know, I guess.

My teacher shoots her a look
        and tells me, *Just be gentle*
        when you tuck in the Lost Boys. . . .
        Wendy is very nurturing.

I look down at Miss Conglin from the stage
        and put my hand on my neck

that feels wider than usual.
Put my hand on my neck
where my throat feels
like it's swallowing knives

and wish someone
was mothering me.

Today is Monday of our
    last week of rehearsing
    before the performance
    Saturday night.
Our first day for dress rehearsal. . . .

I am in a nightgown
    in front of Garrett.
It is long and thick and white
    and buttoned high on my neck.
    But still . . .
    it is a little embarrassing.

He sees me blush and says,
    Are you kidding me?
    So you're in a nightgown—
    I have to wear freaking tights!

And just like that
    he gets me smiling again.
He sees the smile and jumps into

his Peter Pan pose,
fists on hips
and chest held high.
How clever I am! he quotes from his lines.

And I am about to give him
a gentle Wendy-bashing
but I am too tired

and it's not the nightgown
that's making me feel sleepy.

My best friend Taylor is offstage
　　　　in her huge sheepdog costume
　　　　and I see Kelli lean over
　　　　and say something to her.

I can tell Taylor is annoyed
　　　　when she makes
　　　　an elbow-space between them.

After the scene, I ask her
　　　　What did Kelli say to you?

She lifts the shaggy dog head
　　　　so she can talk without shouting
　　　　and shakes out her dark hair.
　　　　She said you were dying out here
　　　　that she should have been Wendy
　　　　that you were typecast
　　　　　　　because you're blonde.

I sigh.　　　All I can come up with is

Wendy's not always a blonde.

Taylor says, *She's an idiot either way.*
You're the best one on this stage.

I wish.

Right now I almost feel
like I'm dying out here
for real.

By the time rehearsal is over
　　my head is pounding
　　and my eyes feel dry-as-the-desert
　　even though my nose
　　has sprung a leak.

Miss Conglin starts to snap at me
　　because I'm taking so long
　　getting my stuff together

　　then she takes a harder look
　　and lays her cool hand
　　against my forehead.
　　Her mouth twists.
　　Someone coming to pick you up?

I nod.

She fingers the studs high on her ear.
Get some rest, Sara.

And drink a lot.
Does your dad keep juice in the house?

I shrug.

Miss Conglin pats me on the back.
See you tomorrow.

But she doesn't sound
like she believes it.

＊ ✿ ＊

Tuesday morning. . . .
In four days I'm supposed to be
        asking Peter Pan
        Boy, why are you crying?

        but my throat is so raw
        I can barely whisper.

Dad has fixed up the couch in the family room
        with extra pillows
        and the daisy quilt Mom made me
        when I was four.

I have the remote control
        a glass of juice
        a box of tissues
        and a phone to call Mrs. Whittier
        from next door if I need something.

I am wishing I could just sleep and not feel
        the head pounding

heat flashing
throat stabbing.

But I hurt too much to sleep.

And my mind is replaying
the way Garrett squirms and laughs
when I sew the shadow
back on Peter Pan's foot.

Who will do that now?

What if his tickled smile
is for someone other
than me?

I keep seeing that smile.

Maybe if Mom was here
    I wouldn't ask her.
But since she's not
    I wish I could ask
    Why do I feel this way?

I can't talk to Taylor
    because she still
    punches boys in the arms
    like that's what they're made for.

And I can't talk to Dad
    because he's Dad.

Already bad enough Mom can't
    see me in my first ever play. . . .

If Mom were here she would
    tuck my stuffed kitty next to me

watch a movie with me

keep my juice refilled

check my temperature

    with her lips

    on my forehead . . .

explain to me about boys.

Wednesday—two days into this illness.
    I am still not feeling better.

Dad had to go to college chapel—
    he was presenting something about
    poetry and spirituality—
    so Mrs. Whittier stayed back.

She has just come to check on me
    when Dad gets home.
    She leans over to take
    the thermometer from my mouth
    her long silver hair swinging forward.

She reads the numbers
    and hands Dad the thermometer.
    You might want to call the doctor
    she says quietly.

She is trying her best not to interfere

so she can stay in our lives.

I know this because it's
exactly what she told me
when I asked where she'd been
lately.

Dad looks at the thermometer,
    mutters, *Still 102,*
        and reaches for the phone.
He pushes my bangs off my forehead
    while he waits for an answer.

        He looks surprised
        by how wet it is.
My freshmen were supposed to come over
    tomorrow night, he says.
    Looks like I'll have to reschedule.

I look out the window
    and across the street
        at the small college campus.

Some crazy kids are braving the March chill
    and having an early water fight

between classes.

I watch a biker duck under
a stream from a water blaster
and land in the bushes
under a girls' dorm window.

I should be sad we'll be missing
the freshman meeting

the only time our house
has life in it.

But right now I
just don't care.

The quick strep test—
        the one where you
        sit outside the doctor's lab
        and feel like a germ factory
        and gag on the swab
        the nurse sticks down your throat—

        comes back negative

        which means it's a virus
        and there's nothing they can do for me
        and I have to just get through it.

Miss Conglin calls
        to ask how I'm doing.

Dad tells her I won't be in school
        for at least another day
        that I'm really not doing well

        and I'm motioning for him to

stop talking
stop making her think
I won't be ready for the play

and he doesn't get it
thinks I want to talk to her

hands me the phone.

Sara?
　　I can hear music in the background
　　something with a heavy beat.
Sara? How are you?

I want to say, Horrible.
　　I want to say, Ready to perform.
　　I want to say, Please don't replace me.
　　I can still be Wendy.
　　I can still fly
　　　　second to the right
　　　　and straight on till morning.

What I say is *Fine*.
　　It comes out a whisper.
　　It comes out a scratch.

Oh, sweetie, Miss Conglin says.
　　Get better.

I'll send Taylor over
with your makeup work.

But we both know
    schoolwork
    is not the real issue
    here.

If I get well in time
> I will be the perfect Wendy.

> I will be so nurturing
> the Lost Boys will miss their mothers.

> John and Michael
> will forget I'm only their sister.

> I will even help Peter Pan
> grow up gracefully.

This is what I think
> when my daisy quilt becomes
> too hot to lie under
> and then not warm enough
> when I'm shaking from chills.

If I get well in time

I will be the best mother.

Even though
I don't have anyone
anymore
to show me
how.

Taylor comes over after school Thursday
    her arms full of books.
    She dumps them on the floor
    beside the couch
       and backs away.
    All the work,
       Tuesday through Thursday.
    If we get more tomorrow,
       I'll bring it.

I look up at her through puffy eyes.
    What's happening at rehearsal?

Taylor softens her
    force-field-against-germs attitude.
    Miss Conglin put in Kelli for now.

Is she any good?

Taylor shrugs.

She knows the part.

I decide to ask Taylor something
    I'm not sure she'd even notice.
    Is, um . . . does Garrett
    still act goofy?

Taylor rolls her eyes.
    He's always a goof.
    Kelli laughs her head off at him.

Just what I was afraid of.

✦ ✿ ✦

It is time for drastic measures.
I need to get well now
    so I can make it
    to the last practice tomorrow.

It used to be our nightly ritual.
    Mom and Dad would come to my room
    at bedtime
    and we'd pray together.

After Mom died
    things were so confused for a while
    and then one night
    I asked Dad to come pray again.

He stood in the doorway for a minute
    then sat on the edge of my bed.
    You start, he said.

But when I prayed
    Bless Mommy and Daddy

a sob burst out of him
then he laid his hand on my head
and lurched out of the room.

I didn't ask again.

So I ask alone tonight
Please, God.

I wake up on the couch
     to sounds in the kitchen.
     Dad?

Just me, Mrs. Whittier calls.
Then she steamrollers in
     with a steaming bowl.
     Hungry?
     Here's some chicken bone soup.

My mind is cloudy with sleep and sickness.
     What day is it?

Friday.   *I've got ceramics lab at noon*
     so one of the college girls
     will be coming later
     to check on you.

I force my zombie brain to think.

The play's tomorrow.

Yes.

    Her drab pottery work shirt
    suits the mood because
    by the sympathy dripping off her face
    I can tell I won't be in the play.
    It is too late

and Neverland

    has a whole different meaning
    for me now.

I'm pretty sure Jocelyn
    was one of Dad's freshmen
    when Mom died.

Now she's a serious senior.
    Majoring in psychology, she tells me
    dark eyes wide with compassion.

She wants to know how I feel
    about everything.
Either I'm too sick to guard my mouth
    or she's going to be
    really good at this.

    Because I tell her everything
    I've been keeping quiet inside me.

I tell her how much I love *Peter Pan* the play
    and how much I like Peter Pan the boy.
I tell her how much I miss my mother

and how my dad's a mess of sadness.

I tell her how lonely I am
    in my own house.

I lumber off the couch
    to show her my room.

She asks about the cats.

There are pictures of cats
on every wall
of my pale-pink room.

Besides my cuddly stuffed kitty,
lions and tigers and cougars
lie helter-skelter on my covers.

Cat-head slippers peek out
from under the bed.

Where's your real cat?
Jocelyn asks.

I don't have one.

She raises her eyebrows in a question.

Mom always said, Ask your father

and Dad always said, No.

She purses her lips and then her look rests
      on my book of Mom Tales.
      What's this?

Mom used to make up fairy tales
      and write them down for me.
      I show her the first page.
      This one's about Mom and Dad.

Beginnings

Once upon a time there was a magical professor who spun poems around his students. The poems gave his students wings. Sometimes they found themselves hovering in the air as if in a dream. One of his students was a girl named for dreams.

Aislinn was born with a hunger for words. She took to the winged poems like she was created to fly. She drank the words in. She swallowed them whole. And she soared.

Each time Aislinn heard the professor speak, her wings grew stronger and she flew toward paradise. But the spell never lasted. When she left the professor, her wings drooped and she drifted to the ground.

She knew she must keep the professor and his magical words with her forever. So Aislinn decided to cast a spell on him.

Her plan was a web of beauty. She reversed the spell he placed on his class and spun her own poems around him. Aislinn's poems captured his heart and sent his soul soaring with dreams of her. And when he was completely under her spell, Aislinn showed him her own dreams of flying with him forever. She offered him the wings of her soul with a book of Love Songs.

The magical professor took the book. He took the book and read her heart and fell into her soul.

The sweetest spell of all.

Jocelyn looks puzzled.
Wow—your mom was a student?

Yeah.　　*They were supposed to live*
　　happily ever after.
　　But there wasn't any ever after.

Jocelyn's grown-up mask slips a bit
　　and she looks like she wishes
　　she didn't know so much
　　about me

　　or that she knew
　　what to say
　　now.

If this were a TV show counseling session
　　now would be the perfect chance
　　to say, Our time is up.

But she doesn't have the

counselor's skill yet
of ending a conversation.

Jocelyn pets my stuffed kitty
pulls at the neck of her sweater
and smiles at me
shyly.

Beneath the fairy tale book
    is a white baby blanket
    decorated with pastel balloons.
I wrap a satin frayed edge
    around my wrist
    and climb into bed,
    too tired to move back to the couch.

Jocelyn eyes the blanket
    and I can tell she's curious

    but this is something
    I will keep to myself.

My eyes close
    the comfort of the silky edging
    touching my skin.

The blanket has been used as
    a belt, a kerchief

a veil, an apron
while Mom and I acted out fairy tales.

Used as a token, a flag
a banner, a snowfall
while Mom read poetry to me
and I dreamed of performing the words.

The blanket was here with me
through it all.

It's still here.
But Mom is not.

＊

I must be delirious
　　　because when I wake up Saturday
　　　I think I can do it.
　　　Be in the play tonight.

I go to the bathroom and open
　　　the drawer that was my mom's.

　　　It's still full of her stuff.
　　　Not like her side of the closet
　　　that only has clanging hangers
　　　since Mrs. Whittier
　　　called my grandparents
　　　to come and help Dad let go
　　　last year.

I rattle through her makeup
　　　and find what I think I need
　　　for the stage.
　　　I shower and do my hair

then play with eyeliner, mascara
powder, blush.

Dad knocks on the door.
Everything all right in there?

I unlatch the door
and let it swing slowly open.

Dad glances in
then freezes.

He looks like he's seen a ghost.

His face scares me
 so I look in the mirror
 to see what he sees.

And I almost see her.
 Eyes defined, cheekbones sculpted.
 If I squint, the messy makeup
 smooths out
 makes me look older.

 So much more like my mom
 than ever before.

I turn back to Dad
 and his eyes change like he
 recognizes me again.
He shakes his head.
 Sorry about the play.
 You know you can't go, right?
 He makes the dorky sad puppy face

that used to make me smile.

I tell him Yes
    and close the door.

Then I watch myself in the mirror
    as the tears start falling

    and I learn too soon
    what happens to makeup
    when you cry.

Grandma and Grandpa call
    three hours before the play starts.
    In my mind
        I can see them
        leaning toward the speakerphone.
    Grandpa listening with his good ear.
    Grandma doing most of the talking.
    Hi, Honey—just wanted to wish you luck
        before your big performance.
    Wish we could be there!
They live in the hills of Pennsylvania
    on the other side of the country.
    Too far away to sense
    my impending heartbreak.

Thanks—but I'm too sick to do it.
    I try to keep the catch out of my voice.

Oh, Honey, Grandma says. *Oh, I'm so sorry.*

What are you sick with?

A stupid virus.
> I tell them all my symptoms
> and they both make sympathetic noises.
> Grandma tells me how sorry they are
> and they hope I get better soon
> and she asks to talk to Dad.

I can tell by Dad's responses
> he feels awkward with them.
His own parents do service work overseas
> so Mom's parents are the ones
> Mrs. Whittier called last year.

I listened from my room
> when they had their face-to-face chat.
The words I heard from Dad were
> *Intrusive.*
> *Handling it.*
> *I need more time.*

The words I heard from them were

Counseling.
Grieving too long.
Not good for Sara.

Now Dad says, *Yes, yes.*
I'm taking good care of her.
I will.

He hangs up and turns to me.
They send you their love.

Somehow   even that small phrase
  sends a tear
  down my cheek.

I try and keep a low profile
        the rest of the day.
Dad is not comfortable with tears
        and I don't feel like
        dealing with him
        not dealing with me.

Now   out there in the world
        the play is going on
        without me.

        A Kelli-Wendy
        is following my Peter Pan
        through the night air.

        Not me.

I lie on the couch
        like an old sub sandwich

forgotten and soggy.

My daisy quilt is damp with tears
and used tissues.

Even the cards
Dad's artsy students made me
are wet from weeping,
the homemade paper wilting,
the inked letters running.

I'm a mess not just because
I'm painfully sick
and missing the play. . . .

There on the TV screen
a sun-bright woman
gently lays her arm
across the shoulders
of her daughter.

My heart wails
and I wonder if she can hear me
from heaven . . .

wonder if she knows
what I'm going through.

It's no use.
I can't stop crying.

Dad comes in with some apple juice
sees my tears
and stops

totally clueless

about what to do.

I feel a sob coming up from my chest
but it startle-stops
when our doorbell rings.

No one is there when Dad answers—
only a little white kitten
who darts into our house
like a paper airplane.

Dad chases it around madly
and they look so funny
I quit crying
and start laughing.

Dad stares at me for a moment
surprised and relieved
and when he finally catches the kitten
he puts it into my arms and says,
Serendipity, Sara.

Someone's brought you a blessing
for a visit.

The little fluffball licks my nose
and suddenly
nothing else matters.

All I care about now
is making this visit
last forever.

Dad has never told me
why I can't have a cat.

He has just told me No
and turned his face away
stared out the window
or into his book
his mouth held
like there are marbles
resting on his tongue

like the marbles
are years of tears

petrified.

Dad goes out the front door.
I hear his footsteps
scrape past the empty carport
then stop.

I picture him
scanning the horizon
searching for the troublemaker
who dropped a cat
into our lives.

By the time he comes back
the kitten is already
kneading a soft spot
in my stomach.

Any ideas who left the cat?
he asks.

I shake my head.

His eyes squint
into his thinking expression

figuring a way
I suppose

to send the cat back.

      ✗ ⚘ ✗

It is lucky for me
     I'm sick and sad.

Now may be my only chance.
     Can't I keep it?
     Please?

The shades come down over Dad's eyes.
     You know cuts aren't an option.

For tonight, at least?
You can't throw it out in the cold.
I wipe at my mascara-running eyes
     and tearstained cheeks
     to remind him
     who he's dealing with
     tonight.

Dad sighs
     looks at his watch.
     I guess it is pretty late.

I can take it to the shelter tomorrow.

I kiss the kitten's forehead
     and it straight-arms its paw
     on my mouth.
Boy or girl? I ask.

Dad sighs again, then checks.
     I think it's a girl.

Maybe looking at the end
     reminds him.
I hope she's litter-trained.
I'd better go find a box
     and some newspaper.

My heart says
     And a way.
          I'd better
          find a way
          that she can stay.

At least she is mine
        for tonight.

I can pretend she'll be mine
        forever.

I'll begin with her name. . . .

She's white as a snowball
        but she's warm
        not frozen.

She's squishy and soft and sweet
        as a marshmallow.

But she's delicate as an orchid
        graceful as a ballerina
        miraculous as an angel.

I can't believe my luck

that she's here with me.

I guess Dad named her
    after all.

Serendipity.

It's been three years.
You'd think we'd be better
  by now. . . .

Dad does the best he can

  but I remember
  cheek-kisses
  soft as velvet.

  I remember
  a gentle voice saying
  It's all right, honey bunny,
  I'm here.

  I remember
  sweet smells and a cushy robe
  when we hugged after her bath.

Tonight in my room

I sprinkle Mom's scented powder
on Serendipity
and I lay my cheek on her side

and I remember

soft.

✦ ❁ ✦

Serendipity is curled on my pillow.
  Her kneading claws
    catch on the eyelet edging
  her throat rattles from purrs
  her head is snuggled into my neck
  so sweet it makes
    my heart hurt.

I think—
  This is what I've been missing
  all these years.

I think—
  I don't want to miss this
  anymore.

I think—
  No is not a fair word
  when you're a kid
  without a mother
  and you need something soft
  to hold on to.

I reach for the phone
	dial Taylor's number.
	Dad would say ten is too late
	but I know Taylor won't care.

She answers so cheerfully
	I have to bury the phone in my quilt.

	She must have had a blast
	being Nana in the play.

	I feel a twinge
	but it doesn't matter as much anymore.
		Shhh, I say.
		This is secret.

What? she asks, suddenly quiet.

How was the play?

Great—what's the secret?

Patience is not one of her virtues.

I have a cat for the night, I say.
     And I need to keep her forever.

Taylor is always ready.
     What do you need me to do?

This is what we work out—
        Taylor will pretend
        her mom is considering
        adopting the kitten.
        She just needs a week
        to think
        to work out the details.

But this will not happen.

Dad doesn't know Taylor's mother
        is allergic to cats.

Dad doesn't know
        if we keep Serendipity
        for a week
        he will get over his No
        because he will fall in love
        with this kitten.

He will get over his No

because he will see
how much
I need her.

He will get over his No.

He has to.

Serendipity has scrambled eggs
      for breakfast
      this first morning.

She is a miracle cure.
I feel well enough for eggs myself.

      Well enough to eat
      at the kitchen table with Dad
      while we watch Serendipity
      nibble near the fridge.

She pats her eggs like they're
      dead mice,
      like she wishes
      they'd get up and run.

Then she chomps them down
      and licks her bowl.

Just like you used to. . . .

Remember?
Dad says
his voice holding memories
of high chairs and laughter.

His hand opens soft
like he's letting
something
go.

As soon as she's finished eating
        Serendipity comes close
        and looks skyward at me.
She gazes with such innocence—
        a baby with one blue
                and one green eye.
My brain tells me to leave her there
        out of Dad's view.
My heart tells me to pick her up.
        I follow my heart.

Dad stares at the fluffy kitten
        washing herself on my lap
        and his eyes close.
He crumples his napkin
        before he's finished eating
        and stands.

        I can tell he's ready
        to be tough.

I can tell he's ready
to break my heart

by taking her away.

I start talking
as quick
as I can.

I called Taylor last night, I begin
      and I tell him how she might
      be able to take Serendipity in a week.
      That's okay, isn't it? I ask
         We can keep her that long, right?

Dad's face closes up.
      Sara, we talked about this.
      The cat goes today.

But she could have a home.
      My voice is squeaking.
      I grab at a statistic I read once.
      Seventy percent of cats
      in shelters die, *Dad.*

Dad clears his throat.
      And what happens if Taylor
      can't take her?
      It'll be even harder for you

to let her go after a week.

I—I'll put up posters, too.
  The first person who wants her
  can have her.
I'll find someone—she's so sweet
  someone will want her.
Dad, I croak out the plea,
  she needs a family.

Dad looks like I gutted him
    with the word *family*.
    Or maybe with the word *die*.
Now I know what writers mean
    when they say *hollow eyes*.

His eyes are like the deep craggy holes
    in broken trees

    and they're pointed
    right at me.

I feel my lip start to tremble   again.

    I think he's going to say No.
    I think he's going to break my heart
        with his own crushed one

    but he puts his hand on his mouth.

He stands up   I think

so he won't have to look at me.

Then he kisses the top of my head
like a surrender.

You're not playing fair, Sara.
He tries for a laugh.
I'll bet you got the flu on purpose.

He doesn't wait to see if I smile.

Dad can't say Yes to a cat
but he also didn't say No.
That's as good as a Yes for now.

My heart starts to lift
until I remember
the dark in his eyes.

And when Dad leaves the room
it feels like
something left the very air
of the kitchen.

The smell of eggs
still lingers
but it's an empty smell.

On the sun-spattered floor
where Serendipity has jumped down
to chase shadows

there is depth
and texture
and warmth.

But here in this breathing space
where Dad left

there is nothing.

I peek around the corner
     and find him at his sad place
     staring at the bookshelves
        poets ordered by alphabet.
Are we going to church this morning?
     I ask softly
     just to say something.

He doesn't turn around.
     One more day to recover.
     You can go to school tomorrow.

Then he reaches out his finger
     and taps the binding of a slender book
     hooks the book and levers it down
     like a drawbridge
     returning
     to its resting place.

I feel fine now, I say
     wanting to move him

in a different direction
like he's moved the book.

He takes the book
without looking at me
goes alone into his room

and shuts the door.

At first the morning feels as thick
as the terrible Tule fog.

I can't stand it when Dad is like this.

He can suck the joy out of a room
in seconds
just by looking mournful.

Sometimes I want to say
She's dead, Dad.
Get over it.

But then I remember
I want something soft, too.

Serendipity changes the air.
She trips and leaps and dodges and twirls
and then falls in my lap to sleep

her face so sweet and fluffy

her breath a gentle stir.

She is good for me.
I know that.

She'd be good for him, too.

Already this morning
　　　she's made herself at home.
She likes to see where she fits in.

I follow her as she
　　　squeezes into small boxes
　　　dallies in open drawers
　　　slithers into sacks
　　　cozies herself in closets.

We play hide-and-seek and I find her
　　　in my boot　　　in my basket
　　　in my backpack　　　in my bowl.

I can pour her like pudding
　　　into any shape of container.

She spreads out soft like Jell-O.

She fills up any mold.

I call Taylor.

  You have to see her.

  She's so amazing.

Taylor says   *I'm supposed to be*

  keeping Mandy busy

  while Mom fixes

    the chicken coop. . . .

Her voice drops in volume.

  We'll bike over real quick, okay?

It seems like Taylor's

  my only easy friend.

  Other girls still look away from me

  whenever a mother is mentioned.

Taylor moved here

  after my mom died.

  Taylor never knew her

  like these other girls did

these other girls who look at me
and what they see is
what could happen
to them.

Like motherlessness
is a disease.

Taylor rides up on an old blue bike
        her little sister trailing behind.
        We can't stay long.
        Mom has plans.

She swings off her bike
        and hauls Mandy wild-haired off hers.
        Where is the cutie-pie?

I turn to show Serendipity's tiny face
        peeking out of my sweatshirt pocket.

Taylor and Mandy both say *Aw*
        and hold their hands out.
I give Serendipity to Taylor
        and she holds her close to Mandy
        so they can both enjoy
        the miracle of kittyness.

She sniffs their hands delicately

a bloodhound looking for clues
about these hands
that hold chickens,
bunnies and ducks.
Taylor's menagerie.

Taylor holds Serendipity like a baby,
wears the kitten on her head like a hat
then hands her to me.
I believe this is yours.

Dad pokes his head out the door
     as Taylor and Mandy
     get back on their bikes.
Taking a test-drive with the kitten?
     he asks them.

Mandy looks confused
     and wobbles on her training wheels.
     Taylor rides between
     Mandy's confusion and Dad's view.
     Yeah, she's a cutie, Mr. James.
     Gotta go, though.
     See you!

Taylor gives Mandy's bike a shove
     to get her started
     and they ride off
     then Taylor circles back
     and hands me a paper
        from her pocket.
     Forgot to bring you
        the assignments Friday.

We would fail as spies.

Someone paying attention

would notice the fishy vibe in the air,

Taylor's nonanswer

to the implied question.

But this one time

Dad's distraction with sadness

works in my favor.

He doesn't notice a thing.

Dad's already closed up in his room
by the time I go into the house.

I put Serendipity
on the back of the couch
and lie down.
I look at the note.

Sara,
- *Start looking for an interesting picture of*
  your family to use as a writing prompt — due
  Wednesday.
- *Middle Ages unit: Read pgs. 131–133*
  in Social Studies book
- *We'll get you caught up on the rest after you get*
  back to school. Feel better!
  Miss Conglin

It really is assignments

not the hoped-for sly note from Taylor
with more ideas on kitten-keeping.

I'm starting to get hungry.
        I go into the kitchen
        looking to see if Serendipity follows.
        She scampers after me
        like a puppy.

        I open some cupboards
        rattle some pans

        hoping Dad will come out
                and feed us some lunch.

I hear his door swing open
>	and his face appears near the fridge.

He's back—all of him
>	not just his sadness.
>	*How does mac and cheese sound?*

And because I spent so much time
>	in front of the TV this week
>	I say, *Super-duper.*

I open the boxes for him
>	and fish out the cheese envelopes
>	while he cuts
>	apple slices for our fruit
>	and circles of hot dogs
>	for the macaroni.

A hot dog circle rolls onto the ground
>	and Serendipity pounces.
I reach down to grab

then decide to let her eat it.
On my way up,
something catches my eye
in Dad's room.
The book he took
is lying in his sheets.
I remember seeing the title
when he pulled it down—
Love Songs.

Now I realize
I've heard that title before . . .
in Mom's fairy tale.

Sometime soon
I must get up the nerve
to ask my dad
a few questions.

The doorbell rings
    while we're still eating.

I hop up to answer
    wiping grease off my fingers
    from sneaking extra bites of hot dog
        to Serendipity.

It's Garrett
    the one I was supposed to be
    flying to Neverland with
    last night.

He looks at me with Peter Pan eyes
    as he hands me a DVD case.
    Miss Conglin asked me
    to bring this to you, he says.
        My dad recorded the play last night.
He looks down like he's reading a note
    on the skateboard at his side.
    Glances up sideways.

Sorry you couldn't be there.

I try to think of something clever to say
      but I'm so nervous
      the best I can come up with is
      How did it go?

Garrett straightens
      strikes a flying pose.
      His stardust hair
      swishes across his forehead.
      We were awesome.
Too late, he tries to look modest.
      See you tomorrow?

Tomorrow, I say
      offhand.

      But I feel
      the same lurch I felt
      that first time in rehearsal

      when he pulled the arrow
      out of my heart.

＊ ✿ ＊

The rain starts after lunch
    drizzling slowly
    down the kitchen windows
    making it warmer inside
    somehow.

    Fortunately
    making the hanging of
    free kitten posters
    impractical
    for now.

We pile on the couch
    to watch the play.

We're like an ice-cream sundae—
    Dad lying on one side
    me on the other.
    Dad ignoring the
    marshmallow
    topping.

Kelli plays a different Wendy
     than I did.
     Older or louder or something.

When Wendy offers Peter a kiss
     and Peter holds out his hand . . .

     Kelli should have paused longer
     before handing him the thimble.

     It would take time to think
     how not to shame him—
     for not knowing what a kiss was.

I watch closely for a while
     hoping to see her make other mistakes
     even though I know that's mean.

I think she got the mothering part down
     but I was more graceful in the flying

and I feel like I was more
Peter Pan's Wendy.

I watch to see if Garrett gives Kelli
the same sweet mischievous glances
he gave me.

The camera is too far away
to tell.

I watch as much as I can stand.
But when Peter hands the thimble kiss
     back to Wendy
     and they turn away
     with tortured looks

     that is enough.

I wanted to share tortured looks
     with Peter.
I wanted to fly out my window
     and get shot down by the Lost Boys.
I wanted to fight with Tinker Bell
     and get captured by Hook
     and walk the pirates' plank.

I wanted Peter
     to fly in my window

    one

        last

           time.

I hit Stop on the DVD
　　and throw the remote.

Dad just looks at me
　　then he pats my leg and says,
　　Well, enough of that, I guess.
He goes into his study
　　muttering something about test grades.

I sigh and slide onto the floor
　　to collect the batteries
　　that fell out of the remote.

　　I had a favorite line in the play
　　when I sprawled leaning like this
　　on the stage.

　　I say it softly, now.
　　Don't go, Peter,
　　I know such lots of stories.

But Peter Pan is gone

and there's no
getting that chapter back.

I throw myself on the couch.

Serendipity bounces up in the air
          from the impact and then
          gets a crazy look on her face.

She races out of the room
          slides around in the kitchen.
          She can't get traction.

          She needs sneakers
          on her slippery feet.

          In an instant she's back.

She takes a mighty leap
          and lands like a Velcro jumper
          limbs splayed

against the side of the couch.

She's stuck.

I can't help laughing,
    she looks so ridiculous.

I wish I had my camera handy.
    I would catch this moment forever
    put it on the mantle

    make it part of our family memory.

Dad leans out of his study door.
     Better start making those posters,
     don't you think?

It's like he can't stand to hear laughter
     in this house

     like he has to squash
     any happiness.

And now I have to advertise
     a free kitten
     to whoever is able
     to keep her.

     Anyone not like me.

This was a stupid idea.

I wonder how I can make Serendipity

seem undesirable.

Impossible.

But there might be
      something I could do. . . .

It comes as a brilliant flash—
        I will make the posters
        with the right phone number
        and show them to Dad.

But when I put up the posters
        I'll change the number one
        to a four

        so anyone
        who dares to call
        will get the wrong number.

        This should foil
        anyone who tries to take
        my slipper-sized kitten
        away.

I surprise myself

with my own deception.
I never used to be sneaky.

But now there's a cat at stake.

A cat who's still stuck
       to the side of the couch.

I take a pretend picture
       and mime placing a tiny print
       across the room on the mantel

       nestled among the rest
           of the family pictures.

I suddenly remember
    the pictures of family life
    I need for school.
I glance back at the mantel
    to see if those will do.

There is a picture of toddler me in a pumpkin patch

    seven-year-old me in a redwood grove

    kindergarten me on Santa's lap

    baby me propped against a teddy bear
    on our same old blue couch.

I unlatch Serendipity from the couch
    and take her with me to look closer.

No pictures of Mom
    no pictures of Dad

only pictures of me
from before Mom died.

In the back of my mind is a memory—
a silver frame set here
that Mom used to change every year
with a new family picture.

I wonder when that picture disappeared.
Where did that family go?

And why am I
the only one
on this mantel?

There are probably digital pictures
        on Mom's old laptop
        but I need pictures I can take in
        and our printer's messed up.

I think I remember a box full of pictures—
        I guess no one around here
        was organized enough
        for photo albums.

The box was pretty
        with roses on the sides
        and it used to sit beside the rocker.

It's not there now.
        Missing, like the silver-framed
        family picture.

No family pictures
        on the family room walls.

Unless you count Shakespeare as family.
The kitchen has pictures of strawberries
        and blue dishes.
The hall has pictures of paths through woods.
The grown-ups in this family are missing.

There are just those old pictures of me.

And a space beside the rocker
        and on the mantel

        where a family used to be.

✦ ✿ ✦

So now I have another question
    to ask Dad
    in the quiet of bedtime.

Not just
    Is that the same book
        in Mom's fairy tale?
but
    Where are the missing pictures?

I have another question
    that will only be asked
    in the quiet of my mind:

    If there are no family pictures

    does that mean
    there's no family?

Dad comes out of his study again

this time carrying his laptop.
I found some templates you can use
for the free kitten posters.

Why is he so eager
        to make this house

        emptier?

By bedtime
 I'm so worked up
 I almost don't even want
 to ask him anything. . . .
 Which question do I ask first?

I cuddle Serendipity
 and wait until he comes to say good night.
I wait until he straightens my covers.
I wait until he whisker-kisses my forehead . . .
 until he stands at the door

then I start with the easy one.
 Dad, that book you were reading today—
 what's it about?

Dad looks at his watch.
 It's a book of poems.

He hesitates at my pointed *And?*

That's a long story, Sara.
I'll tell you more about it later,
all right? It's late. . . .

And now I can't ask
my question about family pictures

because how could that answer
be a short story?

꿏 ✿ ꘤

Our cottage
     is sweet in the daytime
     almost like a gingerbread house.

     Blooming vines climb
     the outside walls

     but they rustle against my window
     in the dark

       and I am afraid
       of their shadows

until
Serendipity appears.

It is hard
     to be afraid of the dark

     when a cat
       is standing on your face.

Dad doesn't have time this morning
      to make scrambled eggs.

He tosses a Pop-Tart at me
      clunks down a glass of orange juice
      thwaps down a container of yogurt
      slides a spoon across the table
         before I have a chance to move.

But what about Serendipity?
      I ask.

He throws his head back
      shoots air out of his mouth
      then shoves a tiny bowl at me.
Run next door and ask for some cat food
      he says.
We'll buy our own this afternoon.

I tuck my kitty into my sweater
      race across wet grass in bare feet

and knock on Mrs. Whittier's door.

I see our reflection in the window.
    I haven't brushed my hair yet
    and it's sticking up wildly
    like Serendipity's head of fur.

We are dandelions of the morning.

Mrs. Whittier opens the door with a laugh
    and clasps her hands together.
    You have a kitty!

For now, I say.
    For a little bit, anyway.

She tilts her head
    sets her silver earrings swinging.
She may know more
    about my father and cats
    than she's ever let on.
You can tell me about it later—
    aren't you running late for school?

Yeah, I say, *but I need some breakfast*
    for Serendipity.

Named her already?
She takes the bowl
    and when she brings it back

Shoji—her tabby—is following her
his eyes on the bowl.

When she gives it to me
    she reaches out the other hand
    as if to smooth my hair
    then draws it back
        without touching me.

May you find a way to keep her, Suru.
    Her solid voice has become soft.
    If there's anything I can do. . . .

Miss Conglin looks up from her computer
    when I put my papers on her desk.
    Good to have you back, Sara
      she says with a smile.
    Did you understand all the makeup work?

I nod.

Did Garrett get the recording to you?

Yes. Thanks.
I wonder if I should say something more
    about the play

    and then three Lost Boys
    and Tiger Lily
    shove through the door
    with their furs and feathers
    all ready to be put away
    in the costume closet

and it seems like old news
that has nothing to do with
empty-handed
me.

I feel the Pan's presence
     when he enters the room.

     The performance has
     left its mark on him.

     A sixth-grade celebrity.

     The air tingles around him
     and when I look his way
     he's almost shiny.

I want to see the smile I saw
     at my door.
I want him to smile at me
     like when I was his Wendy.

But I can't even
     catch
     his
     eye.

Already I'm missing
   the feel of her in my arms.
Six hours is a long time to wait
   for a cuddle.
Six hours of clock-watching
   and busywork.
Six hours of hard chairs
   and hard pencils.
Six hours is too long
   without her.

What will I do
   if she has to go?

Kelli looks different today.
    She's sitting even straighter
    and tossing her shiny hair
    and laughing
    without covering her mouth.

I think that could be me
    if I were glowing from stardom

    but I feel pasty from the flu
    and I have nothing at school
    to laugh about.

Then Taylor raises her fingers at me
    like silly cat claws
    and she grins

    and laughter
    bubbles out of my body
    just as free and light
    as the ting-a-ling
    of a Tinker Bell chime.

Something has happened
     while I've been gone.
It seems to revolve around the thimble
     that Wendy gave Peter
     and Peter gave back—

     a substitute for a kiss.

There is a kind of energy
     in the classroom
     that has to do with giggling girls
     and oohing boys

     and thimbles appearing mysteriously
     on people's desks.

I'm not sure
     if the pretend kisses
     are real wishes
     or just teasing.

But I'm pretty sure

I'm not a part
of any of it
anymore.

Garrett gets up to sharpen his pencil
and I can't help but watch him.
He moves so easily and confidently.

Our Neverland time is over
but yesterday's smile gave me hope
for real time.

Now I'm not sure where
that Garrett went.

I stare at the back of his head
and wonder if his hair
is as soft as my kitten's.

As he passes Kelli's desk
his hand makes a quick movement
and suddenly
there is a folded triangle note
in front of her.

What happened between my Peter Pan
and the Wendy-imposter?

And if not for the flu

would that note
have been for me?

＊ ❈ ＊

When I get home
        Serendipity is waiting for me
        in the window.

I open the door
        drop my backpack
        and give her a quick snuggle.

But something in the air
        is wrong.

No Dad-greeting.

I go through the house to find him.
He is in the kitchen
        kneeling in front of the potted tree
        digging in the dirt with an old spoon
        wearing a disgusted face.

What's wrong? I ask.

That cat, he says
    did her business in this pot.

The kitchen smells bad.
    Not like burned food
    or spoiled milk
    or rotten fruit . . .

    like bad kitten.

Now is definitely not the time
    to ask questions.
But I have to ask one eventually
    after the smell weakens.
    When are we going to buy cat food?

Dad raises his eyebrows at me.
    Do we really want
    to put anything more in
    now that we know what comes out?

Serendipity mews and I take a chance
    hold her up near his face
    and say in a kitty-voice
    Please feed me, kind sir.

Dad smiles with his eyes

    his mouth still holding
    those petrified tears.

We walk to the store
        like we walk everywhere.

        Dad hasn't replaced the car
        since The Accident.

Dad tells me I should
        bring along the posters
        to put up on the way.

        He mentions utility poles
        and bulletin boards
        at the used book store
        and the coffee hangout.

I tell him the posters
        aren't quite ready yet
        and I'll do it later
        with Taylor.

I'm beginning to think
    I really am a good actress
    because he buys it.

Aren't parents supposed to know
    when their kids are lying?

Dad and I slip silently past the stone dorm
    where Mom used to live.

    Two kittens
    are in one window

    looking like fuzzy slippers,
    the same as Serendipity.
    They must be the same age.

Once before when we saw
    a cat in a dorm window,
    Dad told me
    students aren't supposed
    to have pets in their rooms.

I have a funny feeling
 that is Jocelyn's window.

I see Dad notice the kittens,
 blink,
 and turn away

 like he hadn't seen
 Serendipity's family
 watching us walk by.

❦ ✤ ❧

I see Taylor's mom
    in the cereal aisle
    and an awful scene
    begins to play in my mind.

Dad bringing up the kitten situation.
Taylor's mom knowing nothing about it.
Me—busted.
Taylor an accomplice.

Dad, I call
    pointing to something
    in the opposite direction
    like a cliché in a movie.

Dad looks at what I'm pointing to
    and so do I.
It's a tabloid with a headline about aliens
    and a fuzzy green impossible picture.

He looks at me with a question

etched in his face.
It's a where-did-I-go-wrong question
    a that-settles-it
        no-more-stupid-movies decision.

He's ready to lock me in my room
    with books, the old classics.

But it's okay.
Taylor's mom has left the building.

In the pet aisle
	Dad picks out
	the tiniest package of kitten food
	and a small bag of cat litter.

I almost point out
	the price-per-ounce difference
	in the bigger bags

	then I figure that might give away
	my plan for forever.

I reach for a blue litter box
	and Dad tells me
	Put that back.
	We can make do with litter
	and a lined cardboard box
	for a week or less.

I want to say
	If you only knew. . . .

But instead I joke
    The kitten's the one
    who's going to "make doo."
    Get it?

Dad just rolls his eyes
    and shakes his head.

Back at home, Dad tucks the kitten food
        behind the fruit bowl on the counter
        and notices Mrs. Whittier's soup pot
        drying on the drainer.
        Can you take this back
                and thank her? A lot?

Sure, I say.
I pop Serendipity into the pot
        and watch Dad's mouth drop open.
        What could be cuter
        than a kitten in a pot?

But Dad doesn't laugh or even smile.
He turns away.

A heartbeat later it occurs to me—
Mrs. Whittier has lived next door
        all my life,
        has been a big part of our lives
        in the past.

She might know a lot
          she could tell me

          about family pictures
          and why our family
          doesn't look like a family

at all.

Mrs. Whittier takes the soup pot
and croons at Serendipity.
Then she brushes aside my thanks.
Of course, Sara.
I just wish I could do more for you.

And so here is my chance.
Do you think I could
come in and talk?

Mrs. Whittier looks
like I've handed her a gift.
Yes, of course, come in.
Tell me all about this little kitty.

I follow her and kitty-in-a-pot
into the kitchen,
explain how Serendipity
was dropped off.

It's been a while since I've been in here

long enough that I don't recognize
her ceramic pieces displayed on the open shelf
or the bright woven tablecloth
that brushes my knees when I sit.

The usual smell of bread baking
has been replaced by something spicy.

I finish explaining and start to ask

but the question about family pictures
seems too heavy to lift.

I say instead, *Where are your kitties?*

Mrs. Whittier says, *Oh, you want to see them?*
She snaps her fingers in a repeating rhythm
>   and Shoji and Kajiro come running
>   the tabby a shadow
>   to the orange and white Kajiro.

From under the tablecloth on my lap
>   I hear hissing.
>   Serendipity has become an air hose
>   of noisy spitting.
>   Shoji and Kajiro look up curiously.

Shouldn't they be the ones hissing? I ask.

Mrs. Whittier shakes her head.
>   *They're secure at home.*
>   *She's the one who feels threatened.*
She gives her cats a splash of milk in their bowls

as a reward for coming when called.

I lift the tablecloth to pet Serendipity
and calm her down.
She keeps spitting even though
the cats have gone to their bowls.
Why are you being so silly?

She'll be fine once you get her back home.

I put the tablecloth
back over Serendipity's head.
Only if I can keep her.

Mrs. Whittier smiles sadly.
She looks down at her kitties
and I notice they have
new handmade bowls.
How long has it been
since I came to see her?

I'm suddenly ashamed.
Has Mrs. Whittier been as lonely as I have?

I try to remember who she has
        to keep her company at home
        besides her cats.

I know gentle Mr. Whittier died
        sometime after my mom.
Mrs. Whittier has a grown stepdaughter
        who was never very friendly

        but I don't think I've seen her
        since Mr. Whittier died.

I try to think of something to say
        to make up for not visiting all this time
        but no words come to me.

I thank her for the soup

        and make a run for it.

After dinner
>Dad asks if I want
>to look at The Book.
He seems resigned
>to mentioning things
>he'd rather not.

I think I've changed my mind.
>I'm not sure I want to deal
>with difficult things, either

>not right now
>when my visit with Mrs. Whittier
>has made me realize
>there are more empty spaces
>in our lives now
>than the space Mom left.

My excuses are pitiful.
>*I just want a bath*

and to go to bed,
I say.
I'm so tired.

Dad looks surprised
but he nods.

I can feel him watching me
from the corners
of his eyes.

Tonight I discover
     a new form of marine life.

     It is white and fluffy
     and crouches on the edge of the tub.
       A *sea marshmallow*.

She wants to understand water.
     She sticks her tongue under the faucet.
     She watches the waves slosh
       when I scooch around.
     She waits for me to fill her up a cup.
     She likes to drink it warm.

She pats the bubbles.
She leans too far and falls in.

This is more about water
     than she wants to know.

I'm shocked enough
     by the sight of her
     struggling in the deep water
     that I yell   *Dad!*
I toss her out of the tub
     and hide behind
     the shower curtain.

He comes running
     but stops when he sees her,
     tufted legs splayed
     head down,
     miserable on the bath mat.

Stops and laughs.

She looks at him in reproach
     and shakes all over
     so hard she falls down.

Dad grabs a towel

and covers her in it
picks her up like a burrito baby
and roughs up her fur.

You goofy thing, he says.
How'd you get all wet?

She looks wide-eyed into his face
and reaches a sweet paw to his cheek.

Smart girl.

Tonight when Dad comes to say good night
    Serendipity is on my chest
    covered with my old baby blanket.

    The silky edges are frayed
    but the balloons make her look
    ready for a party.

He feels her around the ears.
    She's still a little wet, he says.
    Don't let her get you sick again.

She won't.   *She's nice and warm.*
Serendipity's head sticks out
    just barely from the blanket.
Look how cute she is, Dad.

He looks and his eyes go
    from soft to steely.
    He pins me with a stare
    and he shakes his finger.

Don't get any ideas.
I mean it, Sara.

What? I ask   innocently.

I hear the mumble of his voice
        as he leaves my room.
Don't give away your heart.

Dad trips over Serendipity three times
      while he's getting ready for work—
      coming out of the bathroom
      taking his shirt from the dryer
      moving breakfast to the table.

She has a way of getting under our feet
      like a sheepdog
          herding us toward her bowl
   or a miniature soccer player
          disrupting our goal.

I think it's funny.
Dad doesn't.

I catch him swearing once
      and I shake my finger at him.

      That is the wrong thing to do.

He narrows his eyes at me

and mutters, *Just a few more days.*

This makes him feel better.
It makes me feel awful.

Just a few more days
      is the worst curse of all.

I study my kitten posters on poles
as I'm walking to school.

Taylor and I chose the poles
where it would be hardest for Dad
to see the phone numbers clearly
on his regular route to class.

The changed phone numbers
don't look too suspicious
I hope.

I didn't make a picture
of the cuteness of Serendipity.
That wrong number would be getting
too many calls.

I count the days—
Today, Wednesday, Thursday, Friday.
Will we get Saturday, too?
Four or five days left

for Dad to fall in love
with this kitty.

We need to step up
    the irresistible factor.

Quickly.

We're working on our Middle Ages unit
    and I'm not really listening
    because I can see Garrett
    out of the corner of my eye

    and in my mind
    he's wearing the armor of a knight.

My daydreaming is such a cliché.

Then Miss Conglin gets to Joan of Arc
    and my ears perk up.

    She was so brave and tragic.

Miss Conglin hasn't told us yet
    what the possibilities are
    for our character assignments.

    We will research and role-play
    the type of medieval person

we're given.

Before, I wanted to be royalty.
    But now I think
    Joan of Arc would be

    the greatest role ever.

I must still be daydreaming because
        Miss Conglin says, *Sara*
        like she's already
            called my name before.

She's holding out a folded paper.
        It must be my character assignment.

I open it and read *Peasant*.

        It figures.

I glance over at Kelli
        who is beaming at her paper
        like someone who won the lottery.

        Kelli is probably a noble lady
        and she will ride off with Garrett
        on his steel-footed steed.

My kingdom for a horse.

That horse.
With Garrett on it.

I really need to give my mind
        something else to think about.

Thank goodness for Serendipity.

❧ ✿ ❧

I find Taylor at the basketball court
    at recess.
I saw your mom
    at the grocery store yesterday
    I tell her.

Her face looks like—so what?
    Then she gets it
    and her lips get flat and long
    like when she's making a frog face.
Did your dad talk to my mom?

No. I kept him from seeing her.

Taylor bounces the basketball six times.
    Maybe I should say something to her
    just in case.

Like what?

She heaves the ball at the basket.

Like . . . Sara's got a kitten
she needs to find a home for.
You sure we can't have a kitten?

I nod.

Then at least she won't look clueless
if my dad says something to her.

This is getting too complicated.

I don't like this plot anymore.

After lunch, Miss Conglin says
    Remember, everyone—
    tomorrow I want you to bring in
    at least one picture
    of life with your family.
    We'll be using them as writing prompts
    so having more might help
    if you get stuck.

I raise my hand.
    Do the pictures have to be recent?

Miss Conglin shakes her head.
    No, the age of the photos
    doesn't matter.

I feel like she's purposely
    keeping the compassion
    off her face.

    Like maybe she knows

I wish my family
was normal.

I remember Peter Pan saying,
Don't have a mother.
And me telling him,
O Peter,
no wonder you were crying.

❖ ✿ ❗

I am not going to ask him.

I should not have to ask my father
        where there are pictures
        of my own family.

I should not have to ask him
        why there is no visible evidence
        our family ever existed.

No.   I will find them on my own
        if they are there to be found.

I am not going to beg.
I am not going to plead.

I am not going to do anything
        to make him
                almost
                        cry.

I sneak in the house
        grab up Serendipity
        and let her climb on my shoulder.
I drop my backpack in the corner
        and head out the door.

Mrs. Whittier's is the best place
        I can think of
        to unearth family secrets.

I will pretend
        our last conversation
        was easy.

I will pretend
        I never drifted away
        from Mrs. Whittier's life.

I am pretty sure
        she has forgiven me.

So we will begin again.
Clean slate.

I knock.
She opens the door wide
      gauze sleeves fluttering in welcome.

I step inside quickly.
      What can you tell me
      about after?

Her mouth opens
     but no sound comes out.
Then, *After what, Sara?*

I heave a sigh.
     I need a family picture for school.
     I can't find any.
     They're all missing.
Serendipity creeps beneath my hair
     and I put a steadying hand on her.
     Do you know
     what happened to us
     after . . . my mom died?

Mrs. Whittier stretches her arms to me
     then pulls them back
     then looks at her ceramic-rough hands
     as if willing them to move.

     She sits down on her couch

and pats the leaf-print cushion beside her
then pats my knee as I sit.

I haven't gotten to hug you for years,
        she says.
Do you remember when you used to
        lean against me to get a hug?

I shake my head.

Mrs. Whittier says,
        When your mother died
        all four of your grandparents came.
        You were surrounded by family. . . .
She reaches up to scratch Serendipity
        under her chin and jaw.
        I thought you'd be okay.
Serendipity leans into her fingers
        claws tightening on my shoulder.
        But when they left
        your dad retreated into himself
        and he took you with him.
Mrs. Whittier stops petting Serendipity
        and turns her clear eyes full on me.

Maybe I should have done something sooner.
But I thought you two just needed time
    to lift out of it.
But your dad has never smiled much again
and you . . .
you just disappeared into . . .

She stops.

Into what? I ask.

I don't know.
    Into his sadness?
She shakes her head.
    It would break your mother's heart
    to see you both like this.

Mrs. Whittier bumps me with her elbow.
>   *Remember how she used to sing*
>   *"Put on a Happy Face"?* ·
>   *With that cheesy tap dance?*
>   *She loved to see you smile.*

She teases another memory
>   from way back in my mind—
>   sunlight bouncing off Mom's bright hair
>   as Mom leads me to a backyard room
>   she made from branches
>   wound with flowers and floaty scarves.

Mrs. Whittier remembers it, too.
>   *You called it your fairy castle.*

In my mind, I see a pitcher of lemonade
>   in Mom's hands.
>   *She let me pick blossoms*
>   *for the fairies' cups.*

Of course, Mrs. Whittier says.
> *Your mother got such a kick*
> *out of your imagination.*

Serendipity jumps off my shoulder
> and into her lap
> begging for attention.

Yes, yes, Mrs. Whittier baby-talks to her.
> *She would get a kick out of you, too.*

I wonder if she is just
　　　making small-talk.
　　　Would she really?

Are you kidding?
Your mother would have loved
　　　this little kitty, Mrs. Whittier says.

I sit quietly
　　　heart beating loudly.
　　　Then why? I ask.
　　　Why did we never get a cat?

Mrs. Whittier looks like someone
　　　who has just said too much.
　　　Cornered.
　　　Shifty-eyed.
She shakes her head.
　　　I'm sorry, Sara.
　　　That's something you'll need

to ask your dad.

I consider stomping off in a huff
   but then I won't get to talk
   about Mom.

And I need this.

Maybe Mrs. Whittier is thinking
    about what I'd face
        if I asked Dad.
    I remember once
    when your dad was grumpy
    from grading papers . . .

At the sound of her sudden laughter
    Shoji's and Kajiro's heads pop up
    from where the cats are curled
    hidden behind a trailing vine.

    Mrs. Whittier's plants look like
    she can never bear to trim them.
    They sprawl like
    cats outside on a warm day.

She got you and herself
    dressed up in fifties-style clothes
    and turned on that song from Grease.
She wipes a tear off her laughter.

That one at the end.
And you two danced and sang
on the back deck
for your daddy.

What did he do? I ask.

Don't you remember?
Matthew smiled so big
he looked like his face would crack.

She tells Mom stories
    until my insides feel satisfied
    like eating baked potato soup
    on a cold night.

About the pictures . . .
    I ask finally.
Where do you think they are?

Mrs. Whittier shrugs.
    I'm guessing your dad
    has them somewhere close
    but not out where
    he has to see them
    all the time.

I take a deep breath.
    I'm going to find them.

I'm almost daring her to stop me.

She looks at me steadily
    then holds out her arms

    and I lean into her.

I think I remember this
    after all. . . .

I make my hands like a leash
        around Serendipity's tummy
        lean over and let her feel
                the grass under her toes.

        I'm planning my search
        as we make our way
        slowly back to the house.

It would be easiest to tell Dad
        I need a family picture

        but I want more than that.

I want to see them all.

So when he calls out,
        I have office hours.
        See you at five thirty.
        Mrs. Whittier is on standby,

I make my move
at the sound of the door closing.

His room is his sanctuary
so I start there
in the forest green gloom.
I search under the unmade bed
in his messy drawers
in his closet that twangs
with unused hangers

and behind the abandoned tennis racquets
I find the box stashed way in back.

Treasure.

My hands start to shake
                 so I can barely lift the box.
I take it back to my room.
I don't want to be caught
                 with the rose-covered box
                 in his dark room.

I close my door.
I lift the lid.
I start to cry.

We were a family once.
Here is the proof I remember—
                 Mom with a garland of flowers in her hair
                                  gazing up at Dad
                                  in their wedding photo.
                 Sun-soft Mom cradling baby me.
                 Bright-eyed Dad with toddler me
                                  on his shoulders.
                 So many smiles.

I can't stop looking.

I hear Dad come into the house.
    My alibi is ready.
    I needed it for school.

But he doesn't come to my room.

I decide I will hide the box here
    so I can keep looking.

Dad has dinner ready
        soon after he gets home.

When he calls
        I pluck out one picture
        and shove the box
        in my closet

        almost a mirror
        of where he'd hidden it.

I hear a bump behind me
        and back out quick
        heart thumping

        but it was only Serendipity
        knocking three paperbacks
        off my bookshelf.

I slip the picture
        into my social studies book.

King Tut looks at me
from the cover
slyly keeping mum.

Our family is finally
out of the box

ready to see the world.

I open a new milk jug
        to pour our drinks for dinner.

The plastic ring that sealed the lid
        pops off and rolls on the ground

        a sudden thrill for Serendipity.

She chases
        she pounces
                she swats and sends it flying.
She races
        she bounces
                she puts on a tumbling show.

After a while she calms down
        picks up the circle in her teeth
                and carries it off.

I look at Dad

to see his reaction.

He has just turned back to the stove
  but not quickly enough to hide it:

a tiny grin tilting
  the corner of his mouth.

Dad puts the pot of tomato soup
  in the middle of the table
  with a plate of grilled cheese sandwiches.

While he ladles the soup into our bowls
  I consider.
I'm torn between asking
  once and for all
  why no cats are allowed

  torn between that
  and getting Dad to fall in love
  with Serendipity.

I decide it's smarter
  to go with love.

Serendipity is intrigued
  by the smell of cheese
  and jumps onto an empty chair

then onto the table.

Plan already foiled.

Dad stands to grab the kitten
     but she freaks at his sudden move
     and tears off the table
     and out of the room.

Dad just looks at me

     and shakes his head.

Luckily it's my turn
        to do the dishes.

I'm right near the phone when it rings.

The voice is tentative.
        You don't by any chance
        have a kitten
        you're trying to get rid of,
        do you?

I'm not lying when I say No.

Sorry.   *I saw this flyer and called*
        and the number on it was wrong
        and I thought maybe I saw where
        the mistake was

She apologizes again

and I say it's all right.

But it's not.

What if someone else
         is smart enough to figure it out
         and Dad answers?

Dad calls from his study.
         Who was that?

Just Taylor, I lie.

❧ ❀ ❧

Bedtime has become
 much more fun
 since Serendipity arrived.

She thinks my feet
 are small animals
 burrowing under the covers
  like moles under the lawn.

It is her job
 to stop the moles
 to pounce on the moles
 to wrestle the moles
 until
 they are too afraid
  to move.

She does her job well.

Miss Conglin tells us to put our photos
        at the top of our desks.
Before we start writing
        she lets us walk around
        and see everyone else's pictures.

Garrett's family must like camping.
        He and his little sisters and parents
        are messing around in front of a tent.

Walking further
        I see I am not the only one
        with a broken family.

I forgot how Breanna lives alone
        with her grandmother.

Giselle's pictures
        show two different houses
            her mom in one

her dad in the other.

Jaime has a shot
    of him and his dad
    before his dad was deported.

I guess all families
    have some kind of story.

In my chosen picture
　　　my parents sit on a piano bench
　　　with little me on Mom's lap.

It looks like Easter.

We're all dressed up
　　　and I'm holding a basket.

　　　One of my legs
　　　is flung off to the side
　　　like I can't wait to get down
　　　and find those hidden eggs.

Mom's arms surround me
　　　like she's holding
　　　something precious.

Dad's face shines with twinkling eyes
　　　and a crooked grin.

I glance over at my picture
　　from across the room.

It seems to glow with the promise
　　of a story

　　but I'm not looking for a story prompt

　　I'm looking for something else

　　and I'm not sure what it is.

After we've walked around the room
     we head back to our desks
     to begin working.

I see Garrett stop at Kelli's desk
     and hear them laughing
     about a bulldog in Kelli's picture
     dressed up like a pirate.

Something in me sinks.

I wonder if Garrett knows the dog.
I wonder if Garrett has been to Kelli's house
     like he's been to mine

     only not just there
     to drop off something
        from the teacher.

There because he wanted to be.

Maybe Garrett feels me watching him
because he looks over at me

and smiles.

Oh.

Does he know I like him?

Is he throwing me a crumb?

I look down at my happy picture
　　　but it makes me sad.

I begin writing without thinking.

Once upon a time there was a family.
Then there was none.
Once upon a time there was a mom
who lived and breathed and danced and sang

who loved and dreamed and wished on stars.

Then there was a car.
Then there was a fog.
Then there was the sound of metal
and it was not the sound
of swords and armor
in a story about Joan of Arc
but the crash of a car
as the fog stole the mother's sight

and the headlights of eighty other cars
that piled up like broken sticks
beneath a burning stake.

Once upon a time there was a family.
Then there was none.

I didn't realize a picture
        of a bright Easter morning
        could prompt such dark writing.

I feel like I just burped
        a cloud of smoke.

A hand appears near my picture.
        A finger points to Mom.

        Garrett on his way to the front.

        He lifts a strand of my hair
        that's close to my cheek.
        Two blondies, he says.
        You look just like her.

I stop breathing a moment
        as the sun comes out
        from behind a thick cloud.

Wondering how I should react
to his touch
and his words.

She looks beautiful in the picture
to me.

Is that how I look
to him?

Walking home from school
     I pass Mom's dorm.
The kittens are in the window again.
On an impulse, I climb over bushes
     to tap-play with them
     on the glass.
But the kittens startle at me coming so close
     and one falls into the room.

The curtain moves and reveals Jocelyn
     who widens her dark-fringed eyes.
She pulls open the window.
Sara! How are you?

Good. I motion through the window opening.
     I was just gonna look at the kittens.

I figured.   *How's your new kitty?*

I blink.   I guess she's not keeping secrets.

Great—well—I don't know
if I'll be able to keep her.

She makes an exaggerated frowny face.
        Fingers crossed, right?

Right.

Jocelyn looks back into the room
        then says   *As long as you're here . . .*

Why don't you stay and talk awhile, she says.
Climb on in.

I don't know what my dad
    would think about this
    but I climb in anyway
    twisting past a scrambled desktop
    trying not to disturb a long-legged girl
        sprawled on the opposite bed.
The kittens scatter when I land.
    Where'd you get these kittens?

Their mom was a stray . . . pregnant.
    She got hit by a car after they were born.
    We're still trying to find homes
        for these last two.
Jocelyn waits a beat and
    gives me a considering look.
Do you know if your mom lived here?

I nod.   *Yeah, this was her dorm.*

I thought so.   When I heard your fairy tale
        and I saw her name, Aislinn,
        I wondered if it was the same one.
        That's an unusual name.

The leggy girl sits up.
        Jocelyn. That's not for outsiders.

Jocelyn shrugs.
        She's not really an outsider.
She turns back to me.
        She left an artifact.

My mind goes to old pottery and arrowheads.
        Artifact?

Come on, I'll show you.

Jocelyn leads me across the hall
        to another dorm room.
        Coming through

she says to the occupants.
This is Sara.
Aislinn's daughter.

The girls look up from their books
and gaze at me.
It makes me feel like a zoo creature.

Jocelyn twists a lamp
so that it shines into a drawer.

She pushes aside pens,
index cards, and highlighters.
Take a peek, she says to me.

The inside of the drawer is littered
        with graffiti.
        Dorm tradition, Jocelyn says.
        Girls who get engaged
        while they're here
        put their names in the drawer.

I follow her finger
        to my mother's name.
        She's written
        Aislinn and Matthew.

Jocelyn sighs.
        Isn't it romantic?

She leans toward me.
        Your parents must have been
        secretly engaged.
        It's against the rules
        for a professor and a student

to have a relationship.
She leans back.
    But how can love be
        against the rules?
She shakes her head
    at how ridiculous that sounds.

Jocelyn jumps up all of the sudden.
    Omigosh, I'm late for a test.
She gathers notebooks and pens.
    Don't worry about that rule thing.
    It was a long time ago.
    Things worked out—right?
She flashes me a counselor's smile.
    Gotta run!

She's gone just like that
    and I feel dumb with these girls
        I don't know
    so I drift back across the hall
    half-smile at the girl on the bed
    and scramble out the window

    heading for home

and that rule-breaker—
my dad.

I guess I'm not the only one
who's wanted something
not allowed.

Walking home
    I almost kick myself.
    I could have at least petted the kittens.

Fortunately, I still have my own at home.

Serendipity follows me into the living room
    grabbing at my shoelaces.

There's an empty spot on the bookshelf
    where The Book was.

Dad comes around the corner
    his arms full of sheets
    his face full of disgust.
It's hard to imagine him
    as the rebellious romantic hero.
    Guess where the little monster
    decided to pee   he says.

Um   Uh-oh.   *Your bed?*

Righto.   Heavy sigh.
Any phone calls yet?
    Or what about Taylor's mom?

Dad, I say
    and then I stop.

What else can I say?

I follow Dad to the washing machine.
Maybe you could teach me to do laundry
    I say.

He gives me a double take.
    Why the sudden interest?

I put Serendipity on the dryer
    to let her peek into the washer.
    So if this happens again
    I could fix it instead of you.

Dad narrows his eyes
    shows me which way
    to turn the knobs
    and twist the dial,
    how much detergent to put in.

Then he says
    It's not like she'll be here long enough

to make this a habit.
Saturday morning at the latest.

I clutch her like a baby
    stunned by the real time frame
    and scratch her forehead.
    No, I know
    I say.

But I'm hoping I don't.

Serendipity tries to help us make up the bed
    by standing in the middle of the mattress
    paws reaching as the sheet floats down.
    She dances out of our reach.

Finally Dad says, *Just grab her*
    and I'll do this myself.

I tackle her and pluck her claw-hold
        from the mattress.
    I sit in the armchair
        and hold her on my lap
        so she looks like she's sitting
        like a regular person.

Dad, I say
    to get his attention.

He turns to look
    and I hear his breath go in sharp
    at the sight of us.

He quick-flips the covers
     at the end of the bed
     and the *Love Songs* book
     goes flying toward the dresser.

Dad sees me looking at it.
He picks it up
     and puts it on his nightstand.

I think he's going to say something
     but he doesn't.

With his chin, he holds a pillow
     ready to drop
     into an opened pillowcase.

Dad, I say.

He lets the pillow fall into the case.
     Sighs.
Your mom gave me that book
     to let me know how she felt about me.

So—what's the long story?

He reaches for the book.
      Cradles it in both hands.
      Silent.

Dad, I say, *I want to talk about her sometimes.*
      Couldn't we   talk about her?

He replaces the book.
      His hands drop to his sides.

Serendipity must think
      there's a treat in his hand
      because she springs from my lap
      and claws her way up his pant leg
      to investigate.

Dad yells and pulls her off
      like she's a sticky burr.
He tosses her onto the bed.
That's enough for now.

He's looking at Serendipity
      but I'm pretty sure
         he's talking to me.

I pick up Serendipity
        and take her from his room.

I go into my room and close the door.
Not sure what to do now.

I stand by the door and
        watch Serendipity play hide-and-seek
        with my blankets and quilt.

I can hear Dad finishing up his bed
        then footsteps to his study
        then outside my door.

I wait on my side of the door
        feeling kind of ridiculous.

Serendipity runs to the door
        and paws at it.

A good excuse to open it.

Dad's there
        looking like he got caught
        doing something he shouldn't.
        Looking like he feels silly.

Then he holds out the book
        and a piece of paper.

Here, he says.
>   *I know I should be able to*
>   *talk about her with you*
>   *but I just can't.*
>   *Not yet.*

I take the book
>   and the paper
>   from his trembling hands.

He turns to go
>   then turns back.
He taps the book.
>   *Mom named you*
>   *after how we began . . .*
>   *with Sara's poems.*

He doesn't stay
>   to watch me read them.

It's a really old book.

    Love Songs, by Sara Teasdale.

I wonder if this is a poet

    Dad teaches about

    in his American Lit class.

Inside the front cover

    there's an inscription—

    For Matthew,

        who makes the world

      a poem.

Then the book flips open

    to a poem called "The Look"

    like it's been opened

    to this page

    time after time.

Someone has pasted in

    the name "Matthew"

over one of the original names.

It had to be Mom.

Now with Mom's editing
    the poem says,

      "Strephon kissed me in the spring,
      Robin in the fall,
      But Matthew only looked at me
      And never kissed at all.

      "Strephon's kiss was lost in jest,
      Robin's lost in play,
      But the kiss in Matthew's eyes
      Haunts me night and day."

It's like another artifact
     Mom left behind.
An arrowhead from Cupid.

How did Mom have the nerve
     to give her professor
     a book like this?

He couldn't help but get the message
     loud and clear.

She put it all out there.
I think of Garret and wonder
     if I'll ever be able to do that.

Many of these are not happy poems.
A lot are about death.
I don't know how Dad can bear
     to read this one:

"I SHALL NOT CARE

"When I am dead and over me bright April
 Shakes out her rain-drenched hair,
Though you should lean above me broken-
  hearted,
 I shall not care.

"I shall have peace, as leafy trees are peaceful
 When rain bends down the bough,
And I shall be more silent and cold-hearted
 Than you are now."

No wonder my dad
 has such a hard time

 smiling.

I put the book down
　　　lift Serendipity off my legs
　　　and go to my closet.

I want to see more family pictures
　　　so I can follow where this story went.
　　　How the two of them
　　　became the three of us.

This time I upend the box
　　　and spread the pictures out
　　　like I'm playing with money.

And a patch of orange
　　　catches my eye.

A cat sitting like a little person
　　　on Mom's lap.

I never knew she had a cat.

I look through other pictures in that area
  and find a bunch more
  of an orange cat
  with a tail like a flame.

And pictures of the cat and me
  from baby to toddler.

  Orange cat touching its nose to mine.
  Orange cat leaping into my lap
   on the rocking chair.
  Orange cat cuddled against my stomach
   as we nap on the floor of the den.

No wonder I love cats.

In the last one I find, I'm a tiny baby.

  I'm lying on our blue couch

with the cat on the back of it
looking down at me.

I wish I could remember looking up
and seeing that furry face.

I wish I knew why
a cat was okay before
and it's not okay now.

I think Serendipity
        slept on my head last night.
I can feel puncture marks
        in my scalp
        where she kneaded herself
        to sleep.

Stayed up way too late
        for a Wednesday night
        reading most of *Love Songs*
        and looking at pictures.

Half-asleep
        I step on a piece of paper
        and almost fall over
        trying to unstick it from my foot.

Oh.

It's the paper Dad gave me last night.
        I fell asleep and forgot about this.

I should be getting ready for school

but I have to stop and read it.

SMALL DEMANDS

For two days now
the child has appeared
when I've reached the best part of a novel.
She places herself between me and the words
her chubby hand planted on the page
like a bagel with fingers. . . .
The bagel will not be removed.
I try lifting it gently, at first,
then I grasp her wrist
then I pry at her palm
but she quickly frees herself
and slaps her heavy hand back on the resolution.

It will have to wait.

She senses I have given in
and settles sweetly into my lap
pointing to numbers on the page

and reciting them.
She turns pages and asks for words
eyes bright with my attention
fingers light with learning.

Every cat I've owned has refused to budge
from a newspaper spread out on the floor
in front of an anxious reader.
But cats can be shut behind doors.

I have a child.
The story will wait.

She loved me.

I mean, I knew that
        and I felt that
        and I remembered that.

But here is more evidence

        and at the same time
        I'm teary with love
        I'm angry with Dad.

Why didn't he give this to me sooner?

Why is he so wrapped up
        in his stupid grief

        that he won't let me
        have my own?

I am storming out of my room
        with cat pictures
        and the poem
        when my foot kicks
        the *Love Songs* book.

I honestly need to stop
        dropping things on the floor.

I pick up the book
        and like black-light lit fingerprints
        I can see Dad's tenderness
        all over it.

The book
        melts me
        toward Dad.

Less stormy now
        I take the pile of artifacts

to the kitchen.

Dad has toasted me a waffle
     and cut me a grapefruit
     and is heading out the door
     with his leather schoolbag
     and a backward wave.

Wind out of my sails.

Before I leave for school
　　I go into Dad's room
　　with evidence.
I want it to stand out
　　so I make his bed.

I wonder if I should put the lone pillow
　　in the middle at the top
　　even though he still sleeps
　　only on his own side.
Maybe this is why
　　he never makes his bed.

I place his pillow on his side
　　and center a picture
　　on the pillow.

The picture is of me—
　　baby on a blue couch

with a furry guardian angel.

He'll wonder how I got the picture.

I wonder if he'll be mad.

But he'll know
     that I know

     cats were not always
     forbidden.

It seems pointless
    to hide the pictures now.
I leave the pile in the middle of my floor
    and close my door
    against Serendipity
    so she can't ruin them.

I have one picture
    in my sweatshirt pocket
    to have it near me.

It's of me and the orange cat
    looking out the front window
    along with a reflection of my mom
    taking the picture.

I wave good-bye to Serendipity
    looking out the same window.

Mrs. Whittier is in her front yard

doing something with flowers.
I jog over to her.

Good morning, Sara!

I know something I tell her.
  I pull out the picture
  and show it to her.
But Dad's still not talking.

Mrs. Whittier nods gently.

I turn and head for school.

Miss Conglin tries to relate
          subject matter to our lives.
So she brings back the thimble kiss.

A metaphor, she says during writing time,
          uses one word to stand for another.
She steps forward
          grabs the thimble off of Ana's desk
          and holds it up.
Just like Wendy, some of you in class
          have been using a thimble
          to represent a kiss.
She holds up her hand
          against the outburst of silliness.
You've been using a metaphor.

Well   I haven't used this metaphor,
          because I am thimble-less.

I glance at Garrett
          off to my left.

He is doing some kind of magic trick
     where he can make his thimble
     disappear and reappear.

No one's listening to Miss Conglin
     who's moved on to similes.

Our minds are on metaphors.

Taylor has a peasant assignment like me
      so we research together in class.

I slide the picture out of my pocket
      and show it to Taylor.
      Notice anything off in this picture?

She takes the close-up
      and says   *Ha   look at that.*
      A cat.
      I thought cats weren't allowed.

      I thought so, too, I say.
      My dad's got some explaining to do.

Taylor hands me back the picture.
      New plan?

I don't know.

I'm just winging it
right now.

She taps her pencil on her notebook
   ticking down the minutes.
   Time's running out   she says.

Believe me—
   I don't need reminding.

Sitting too long is hard for Taylor.
When Miss Conglin is busy,
        her back turned,
        Taylor stands up
                and holding the page
                she's been working on
                in one hand
        she does a mini peasant
        dance and song.

I have no soap
My bed is hard
My bread is smeared
with greasy lard
I have no bath
I'm full of fleas
Someone, won't you
help me, please

Something nags at my mind

as I'm laughing.
Hey, Taylor, do you know
any of the songs from Grease?

Taylor shoves me.
   That's not the kind of grease
   I was singing about.
   But yeah   I know them all.

I tell her why I want to know
   and she says
   Come over after school.
   I've got the DVD.

Taylor's house is the opposite of mine.
There is honest-to-goodness life here.

First we visit
      the chickens and ducks in the coop
      and the bunnies in their cages.
Then Taylor lifts Mandy
      by an arm and an ankle
      and swings her around like an airplane.
Then Taylor's mom gives us cookies
      fresh from the oven.
Then we dance like hooligans
      in the family room
      to the great songs from *Grease*.

It's awesome.

Until we get to the end of the last song
      the one Mom and I sang for Dad.

I can't believe the lyrics.

The happy crowd is singing
We'll always be together
on and on and on.

Taylor notices I've stopped dancing
and I see the moment when she gets it
in a ripple across her face.
Um, you want to go outside
and hug a bunny?

Yes.   I do.
And then I want to go home
to Serendipity.

I'm at my front door
        when I hear Mrs. Whittier calling.

Sara,   *wait.*

Serendipity has already seen me
        from her spot in the window.
            Her mouth opens in silent mews.
I put my hand on the glass and tell her
        Just a minute, Dipity.

Mrs. Whittier is holding a CD.
        My stepdaughter's
                finally coming to visit.
        I found this while I was
        cleaning out the guest room.

I probably look as clueless as I feel.

When you were little
        and I sat for you at night

I'd play this CD
your mom made you for bedtime—
it's her voice telling you fairy tales.

I feel a tickle of a memory.

Mrs. Whittier twists her mouth around.
> *I shouldn't be the one telling you this*
> *but you know about the cat now*
> *and Matthew can't seem*
> *to talk about it.*

I have no idea what that
has to do with fairy tales.

Then she tells me how the cat died
because they didn't notice an infection
until it was too late

and how guilty Mom felt about it

and how she cried for three days.

That was the cause for no more cats.

And when I got old enough to start asking
        for a cat of my own
    that was the reason the cat pictures
        were hidden.
   That was the reason one fairy tale
       could not be played
  and why it was removed from the book.

They didn't want me to think
    cats were a possibility in this house.

Wait   I say   *What good would that do*
  if I already knew about the cat?

Mrs. Whittier shakes her head.
    You were two when that kitty died.
    You'd forgotten about him by the time
       you asked for a cat.

She hands me the CD.
    The cat fairy tale is the first one.

I can't believe I'm holding
　　Mom's voice in my hand.

Go on, now　　　　Mrs. Whittier says with a smile.
　　You know you want to.

I make a dash for my CD player
　　grabbing up Serendipity on the way.

Dad is still safely at school.

I drop in the disk
　　and settle us on my bed
　　　　my kitty curled in the center
　　　　of my crisscrossed legs.
All I have to do
　　is push the button
　　to hear my mom's voice.

I'm almost afraid to do it.

Listen, Serendipity.
This is my mom.

Mom's voice tears my heart
   when she starts.
   Okay, honey bunny,
      snuggle down.
      Here's your story.

Once upon a time a princess lived in an ivy-covered tower. The tower walls were hard, cold stone. From her window she could see a meadow where furry creatures played in the sun, and she longed to cuddle their warm, soft bodies. But the rule-keepers had forbidden animals. No creatures were allowed inside to comfort her.

The princess was lonely.

One night, she heard a cry from below. She tiptoed down the stone staircase to find out who made the sound. She peeked outside the door into the dark. At first, she saw nothing. There was no one on the doorstep. The bushes held their secrets. The princess called out into the night, "Someone, someone who is scared, I am here. Come to me."

The bushes trembled and rustled and frightened the princess. But she remembered she was lonely and she became brave again.

She called, "Someone, someone who is scared, I am here. Come to me."

And this time the bushes answered her with a quavering mew, and a furry creature tumbled out and poked a nose at her outstretched hand. He twined his tiny body around her ankles until she picked him up and held him in her arms.

She remembered the rules about creatures. But the kitten creature was scared and alone and she was brave and alone. So she brought the kitten to her tower room and kept him there. And they were happy.

But it wasn't long until the rule-keepers heard about the kitten and demanded she turn him out. The princess couldn't bear to lose the kitten. So she wove a magic rune, a spell to make him invisible.

This worked for a while. But the kitten was playful. One day he saw the rune beckoning like a string and he pounced on it. He worried it until the rune unwound and floated out the window. It landed on the shoulder of a rule-keeper, who looked up to see where the rune had come from. He saw the kitten in the window.

At the same time, the princess noticed the kitten was no longer cloaked by the rune. She ran to get the kitten out of sight and looked out the window to make sure no one had seen. Below was the rule-keeper, watching. The princess didn't notice he was smiling. She only knew he had seen the forbidden kitten. Thinking all was lost, she fainted.

When the rule-keeper saw the princess faint, he rushed into the tower and up the stone stairs. He cradled the lonely princess in his arms and murmured comforting words to the kitten. When the princess awoke she was overwhelmed by his tenderness. The rule-keeper in turn was captivated by her heart. He invited the princess and her kitten to live in his warm cottage where there were no rules against furry creatures. The princess and the kitten joyfully accepted his invitation.

And they all lived in the cottage happily ever after.

Now close your eyes, honey bunny
and dream of sweet things.

I am full
    with the sound
    of Mom's voice.

But in the silence that comes
    with the ending of her story
    I have this thought—
        The rules are back . . .

    and I hear a noise.

I glance toward my open door
    and catch a glimpse
    of Dad turning away

    catch an echo
    of Dad retreating
    once again
    to his room.

How much did he hear?

It wouldn't matter.

He could fill in the gaps
    of his own story
    told in the voice
    of his dead wife.

I should have closed the door.

Now I regret
 leaving the picture
 of me and the orange kitty
 in his room.

He will go in there
 with her voice in his head

 and see evidence
 of my prying and accusing.

He may never want to talk to me again.

I want to go to his door
 and test this out.

I want to hear him say
 he loves me anyway.

I am too afraid to ask.

Dinner is saved
        because he has his phone
        in his room.

I wondered what we'd do for dinner
        if he never came out

        but he has solved that problem.

The pizza guy rings the doorbell
        and Dad opens his door
        a slit.

Use the money in the jar, Sara.
        I'm not feeling well.
        Help yourself.

That's usually a phrase directing you
        to serve yourself some food.

But this time, it feels wider:

Help yourself, Sara
because Dad
can't help you now.

The pizza
       usually a happy food
       tastes hard
       and uncaring.

After pizza
        I drift back to my room.

Dad's door is still closed.

I'd like to hear Mom's voice again
        but I'm afraid Dad will hear
        even through closed doors.

I pick up *Love Songs*.
There are a few poems at the end
        I never got to
        so I read them now.

And the last one I hear in Mom's voice.
I can remember her reading this to me
        many times.
Maybe it was her favorite.

Here is the best line:
        "I think that every path we ever took

Has marked our footprints in mysterious fire,
Delicate gold that only fairies see."

She made magic for me.
I don't want that to end.

For no good reason other than
　　　　I'm just sick of this sad house—
　　　　I desperately want to storm
　　　　the prince's castle.

　　　　But I've already burned
　　　　　　that drawbridge.

Serendipity leaps from nowhere and lands
　　　　on the open pages of *Love Songs*
　　　　pressing claw marks into the paper.
I gasp and push her away　　　*No!*

She looks surprised and scared
　　　　and I suddenly remember . . .

Tomorrow is my only day left
　　　　to woo the prince

　　　　and he's locked up in his room.

❖

It occurs to me as I'm walking
    lonely to school . . .

    if Dad doesn't fall in love by tonight—
    by tomorrow morning
    Serendipity will be on her way
    to the shelter.

That was the deal.
Well, Dad didn't know about
    the falling in love part

    but as far as he's concerned
    today is my last chance
    to find her
    a home somewhere else.

I am past panicking about losing her
    and starting to realize

    I could be responsible for

letting her end up
at the shelter.

She might die because
I brushed off a phone call.

And it will be my turn
to cry nonstop.

Miss Conglin announces a special treat.
     We will watch a DVD this afternoon—
     our production of *Peter Pan*.
She's brought popcorn
     and pillows for us to sit upon
     on the floor.

This day just keeps getting worse.
     Serendipity is in peril
     and now I'll have to sit through
     that whole painful performance.

I'm moaning to Taylor at recess
     and Kelli hears me.
     She swishes by and says
     Too bad you missed it, Sara.

Not too bad for you
     I throw back at her.
It's supposed to sound like a joke
     but I get my voice wrong.

It sounds like an accusation
>like my words are pointing fingers.
>I can feel the just-kidding look
>fall off my face.

So I say it instead:
>*I'm just kidding.*
>*Really.*

But I sound like a mean girl.

Kelli flips back
>*What's wrong with you?*
>*You won anyway.*

I have no idea what she's talking about.

I turn to Taylor and she looks
>as confused as I do.

Taylor gets her Harriet-the-Spy look
>and says, *I'm on it.*
She casually walks over to
>a group of Kelli's friends.
She's back in no time.
>*Remember that note you told me*
>*Garrett gave to Kelli?*

I nod.

He was answering her do-you-like-me note.

He checked "I like someone else."

Hope flares.

He didn't say,
but they think it's you.

Maybe this day isn't so bad
after all.

Garrett sits in the second row of pillows
and there is an empty pillow
in front of him.

I don't wait for someone else to sit there.
I remember how my mom
made things happen
and I think maybe
I can do that too.

I try to be casual.
I sit in front of Garrett
like I don't notice he's there.
I can see his straggling foot
out of the corner of my eye.

I put my hands behind me
like I'm going to lean back
and my fingers brush his shoe.

He jerks it back.

I look behind me   grin.
          Foot still ticklish?

And then I see that slow smile come
          like a sunrise on a lake.

Beautiful.
Too bad I have to face forward.

I decide the best way
  to get through this performance
  is to imagine myself
  in the role.

I manage it all the way to the end
  when Wendy is grown up
  and her daughter says of Peter
  He does so need a mother.

And Wendy says, *Yes, I know.*
  No one knows it so well as I.

Just then a piece of popcorn
  sails over my head
  and lands in my lap.

I look behind me at Garrett
  mock-studying the ceiling

with a smile twitching
at the edges of his lips.

He's underlining the end.

Because there on the screen
    is the whole cast
    taking in applause and
    holding up a big sign that says
        For Sara!

That image warms me
      as I'm walking home from school.
      It overlays a cold feeling.
      How can I get Dad
      to fall in love with Serendipity?

Maybe I could soften him up.
I try to remember what kinds of things
      used to make Dad happy.
I flash on pictures from the box
      where we're hiking in Yosemite.
      He loved walking through the trees.

We haven't done any hiking
      since Mom died.
We don't even have a car to get us there.
But he does love trees. . . .
      I could make him a tree picture.
      I could get him a tree seedling.

I could . . . none of this has anything
to do with Serendipity.

I'm feeling hopeless   until I slip my hands
into my jacket pockets.

I remember Garrett's quick hands
when my fingers close
around a familiar object.

A thimble.

Warm again.
I remember Mom's inscription
    about Dad—
    "who makes the world a poem"—
    and I think Yes.
    I am holding a kiss in my hand.

I keep the thimble tucked in my palm
    to give me strength
    when I face Dad inside.

Dad's bedroom door is open.
His leather bag is gone.
A short note on the kitchen table.
    Mrs. Whittier is home
    if you need her.

What I need is Dad here and a miracle.
Serendipity comes running
    stretches her paws out toward me
    her back end high in the air.

Then she drops loudly on her side
and rolls over to show me her tummy.

So cute.   Dad needs to see this.

I rub her tummy, then go to my room
    to find a nest for the thimble.
    I'm trying to think of some special way
    to show Garrett how I feel
    when I see—

    there on my pillow
    a stack of papers
    in Mom's handwriting.

    More of Mom's poems.

As I page through them
    it strikes me
    they're all about cats.

I pick up the first one to read.

SONNET FOR A CAT AND HER KITTENS

The musty-sweet smell of hay is in your
fur, kitty. A hint of where you've hidden
your babes. I know strangers are forbidden
to linger near the sun-dappled nest or
stroke the tiny tender noses before
you allow it, but I've watched your children
tussle in the night. Am I forgiven
if I explain that your son has a roar
like a dragonfly, and your daughters grow
more like you every day? Their faces draw
me; I can't help but climb up to the loft
while you're away and watch them swaying low
in their walk, or curling up on the straw
to sleep. They are my joy; so clean and soft.

I pick up another one. . . .

CATNAP

The cats are curled
like cinnamon buns
on the floor

like you could take
a giant spatula
and lift them
onto the plate
of your chair

like their sweetness
would sticky
the flat of your hand

like the steam
of their warmth
would rise
in clouds
of aromatic
dreams

I keep reading
        until I'm cat-saturated.

It's hard to believe
        she wrote
                this many poems
        about cats.

It's hard to believe
        I didn't know
        this side of her.

Does this Dad-offering
        mean I'm forgiven
        for making him sad?

I guess he's reaching out
        the best he can
        right now

sharing a bit of Mom
with me.

I wonder if he'll tell me
in his own words
why we can't have a cat.

Unless maybe these poems
are supposed to be
his silent answer.

Because she loved them.

Inspiration hits.
  I am a poet's daughter.
  Maybe I can convince my dad
    through a poem
    that we need this cat.

I try to think of how I can write
  all the reasons in a poem.
  But my mind and the page
    stay blank.

Serendipity mews near the window
  and an idea bursts in my head.
Maybe a field trip
  will start my brain working.

I grab a notebook and pen
  tuck Serendipity under my arm
  for her first trip

to the backyard.

Right away
    when I set her down
    she rolls in the dirt.

She's not exactly
    the princess type.

But at least I get
    a warm-up poem out of it.

A TRIP OUTSIDE

Maybe if you weren't
so white
I wouldn't know when you got
so dirty.

You look like a cloud
that is thinking
it ought to rain.

You look like a marshmallow
dunked in hot chocolate.
and dropped in the dirt.

You look like a pile of socks
someone should put
in the wash.

I thought I only
  took my eyes off Serendipity
  for a second

  but when I look up from the page
  she's gone.

I scan the yard.
  I call her name.
  Does she know her name?

I walk the edges in a quick-step
  looking behind bushes
  up into trees.

How could she disappear
  so quickly?

I think she's too little
  to climb the fence
  but then I see something

that makes my heart bang:

a kitten-sized hole in the fence
the side that leads
to the front of the house
and the street.

She could be anywhere.

It's close to dinnertime.
    Somehow the light changed
    while I've been searching.

    No sun.
    The gray of dusk is closing in
    and a feeling of impending fog.

I race out the gate
    for a quick look in the front yard
    but no one is there

    no little white shape
    to turn and greet
    or even startle and dash

    only silence and emptiness.

Dad! I start to yell

before I even get in the front door.

I find him in the kitchen.
He turns with the phone in his hand
and a strained expression on his face.

I can't find Serendipity.

He doesn't seem to take this in.
*When were you going to tell me
that Taylor wasn't taking the cat?*

What?

He hangs up/bangs up the phone.
*Taylor's mom just called to say
you left your sweater at their house.
I asked her if she'd made her mind up
about Serendipity
and she thought I was kidding.*
He throws out his hands.
*She's allergic, Sara.
There was never any chance
they were going to take the cat.*

I'm not sure which disaster is worse —
    Serendipity's disappearance
    or the uncovering of the plot.

Dad, she's gone.

Dad looks at me
    then shuts his eyes.
    I can't abide lying
    he says.
    Maybe now
    things will get back
    to normal.

I can't believe what I'm hearing.
Normal? You want things back to normal?
I can feel my voice rising
     like a crazy person's.
What was so great about normal, Dad?
     I don't remember that
     making you happy.

Dad's face drops, but his eyes stay stern.
     She is not your cat.
     You knew that from the start.
     How could you sneak around
          behind my back?

That is too much.
     You're a great one for talking
          about sneaking around.
     I know about you and Mom.

Dad closes his eyes like he has a headache.

You're a child.
You don't know anything.

That's because you won't tell *me anything!*

He shakes his head hard and turns
     the usual cowardly direction
     toward his room.

It's becoming clear—
     he's not going to help me find her.
     He doesn't care if she's lost forever.
     He doesn't care how scared I am.

I reach for the doorknob
I will go outside
     and find her myself.

He hasn't done
     his standard disappearing act yet.
     Sara, he says, *go to your room.*

My mouth drops open.
     No, I have to find her.

Go to your room.   *Now.*

I think my heart has just become
    a dumping place
      for sharp and heavy rocks.

How can he be so mean?
    She's lost.

What's so wrong about wanting
    a cat in my life?

I shouldn't have to lie
    in order to get one.

Serendipity is lost
    and I'm being sent to my room?

I stand at my window and look out on the street
      hoping that I'll see her.
But even the trees are disappearing
      in the fog.
Soon I won't be able to see anything.

It's another stupid Tule fog.
Well, I'm not going to stand here
      and let it kill Serendipity, too.
I'm not going to stay here
      while she's out there
      alone.

My dad showed me
      how to remove the window screen
      in case there was a fire.
Knowledge is as powerful as fairy dust.

      I'm gonna fly.

I try not to think of the trouble
    I'm going to get into.

I'm not sure what's happened to me
    since Serendipity showed up.
I used to do everything my dad told me to
    just to keep him from losing it.

But things are different now.

I feel like Joan of Arc.
    I know I'm on the side of right.
    I won't give in
    even if I'm burned at the stake.

Fortunately, that's not going to happen.
I'll probably just be grounded
    for the first time in my life.

But it will be worth it

because I will know
I've put someone else's life
before my own.

Someone soft and sweet
who needs my help.

I will be a hero.

I struggle a bit with the screen.
I hope Dad can't hear me.

When the final clip is turned
I pull the screen toward me
and lean it against my bed
leave my soft pink room
for the spooky night.

It's easy to climb out of the window
no prickly plants to scratch me
no leap to the ground
since it's only one floor
no shaky rainspouts to climb down.

If I were my dad
I might think about planting a rosebush
right here
so it wouldn't be so easy

for my daughter
to escape.

As I slip out the window
I see the fog slipping in. . . .

I start with a wide sweep
        around the fog-shrouded yard.

    No Serendipity.

I look toward the street
and hope-pray she's still close by.
I need to look deeper.

I'm searching under the bushes
        at the side of the lawn
        chanting, *Please, God*
        please, God   please, God
        when I hear Dad's voice
        coming through my window.

Sara? And then he must have noticed
        the open, screenless window frame
        because his voice sounds panicked
        as he calls my name out into the dark.

And I realize he can't see me
through the blanket of fog—
has no idea how far I've gone.

Maybe he thinks I've run away from home.

My gut tells me, Answer him
but my brain says, No.
If I go in now, I won't have Serendipity
and I'll still be in trouble.

I keep searching.

Fog water collects on the leaves and washes my hands
as I rifle the bushes hoping for a glimpse
of bright white.

My sweatshirt sleeves and my tennis shoes
are getting wet
making me feel cold and squishy.

I focus on finding Serendipity.

Still   I can't help but hear him.

I can't help but hear him
     crashing out the front door
     his footsteps racing away from me
     toward Mrs. Whittier's lit-up house.

He knocks normally at first.
     I can imagine him
     trying to keep it together
     trying to be calm and rational.

     But Mrs. Whittier doesn't answer
     and soon he is banging on her door
     and calling out to her.

Still no answer.
She must have left lights on
     when she went
     to pick up her stepdaughter.

Dad stops banging and shouting

but I can hear him breathing hard

and I hear him gasp, *Sara*

and I hear him pounding to the curb
and calling my name out through the fog
louder and louder
in his terrible panicky voice.

Sara, he cries over and over
and something in my chest cracks

but I stay stubbornly by the bushes
and think of Serendipity
and how much she needs me.

Then I hear Dad moan
Not you   too

and that is more than I can bear.

I run to his voice.
Daddy, I'm here.
I'm sorry.

＊ ❁ ＊

He wraps me in his arms
      and breathes *Thank you*
      into the top of my head
      only he's not talking to me.

      And he sobs like I haven't heard
      since those hopeless nights
      the first few months after Mom died

      and that makes me cry.

      We're an awful wet mess together
      sodden by the heavy fog
      and our tears.

Don't ever do that again, he gets out
      and I shake my head.
Never, don't ever do that again.

I won't.

He pulls my face up in both hands.
Why is that cat
so important to you?

It's not just the fog
that feels like it's suffocating me.
I tell him the hard truth.
I get so lonely, Dad.
I need someone to hold on to.

Dad's whole body seems to droop
and I realize I'm finally telling him—
he hasn't been there for me.
He sighs and reaches his arm
around my shoulders.

Then he walks me through the fog
back into the house.
There's something
I have to tell you.

Dad sits me down on the couch.
>   *Your mother died*
>   *driving in fog like this.*

I know, Dad.

He puts up his hand like a stop sign.
But you don't know about before. . . .
We had a special cat—that orange one.
When MacLeish died—
He closes his eyes.
Mom cried for three days.
>   *I didn't ever want to*
>   *go through that again.*
So for years when she brought up
>   *getting another cat*
>   *I just refused.*
Dad looks at me.
Your mom finally convinced me.
And she wanted to surprise you.

She was on her way to get a kitten
when the accident happened.

That explains a lot.
Now I miss her even more.

But wait.
Dad, she wanted us to have a cat.

Dad nods.
This is what I'm telling you.
He's quiet for a minute.
I'm also telling you
why I couldn't have a cat here. . . .
I thought it would remind me too much
of what I lost.
I thought having a cat without having her
would be too hard.

I don't want to ask but I need to know.
Is it?

Dad's voice cracks.
It's hard, Sara.

This is a tragic story
      and the rocks in my heart get sharper
      but I can't help but hear
         he didn't say   *Too hard.*

Does it make me a bad person
      to hear hope
      while we're talking about
      my mother dying?

Dad, I start
      but I don't know what to say.

He gets up for a box of tissues.
When we're drier   he says,
      She's scared and hiding right now.
      I doubt we'd ever find her tonight.
      But tomorrow. . . .

This is not a good time
        to argue.
I wasn't finding her outside
        anyway.

I stare at Dad
        afraid to ask.

He stares back.
        You were wrong
        to lie to me, Sara.
        And you were wrong
        to look through my things.
        And you were wrong
        to leave your room.

        But I was wrong, too,
        not talking about Mom
        not letting you have a cat.

I wait

hoping, hoping.

Your punishment is
    you are grounded for two weeks.
My punishment is
    you can have a cat.

I jump into his arms.
    I love your punishment,
    I tell him.
    Thank you, Daddy.

❧ ❀ ❧

I can finally have a cat
        but the one I want
        is gone.

Dad tells me not to worry
        but how can I not?

She's a baby
        out there alone.

I finally drift off to sleep.
        Am I dreaming?

She is calling at the back door
        and sharpening her claws
        on the doorjamb.
She wants in so badly
        she flings herself
        like sticky tape

at the screen door
claws hook and hold

and she is stuck
clinging
hanging
singing a sad song

impossible to ignore.

I wake up suddenly.
Was I dreaming
        or did I really hear something?

I go out to the kitchen
        and there in the morning light
        hanging on the screen door
        is Serendipity.

Serendipity!
        I run to detach her.
        Her body swings out
        when I open the door
        but she is truly stuck.

Dad comes to the rescue
        lifting each claw
        from the tiny steel squares.
See? What did I tell you?

She knows a good thing
when she sees it.

I cradle Serendipity in one arm
and use the other
to give Dad a hug.

I know a good thing
when I see it,
too.

How to hold a sleepy kitty . . .

. . . in the nap of your arm

near the crook of your dream

in the armchair of your tenderness

on the pillow of your heart. . . .

It's maybe six months later. . . .

Dad hands me one of the tennis racquets
  that live near the front door—
  within easy reach for our game time.

We leave the lights on in the family room
  to welcome us when we return
  and wave at Mrs. Whittier
  through her picture glass window.

We walk past Mom's dorm
  in the campus dark.

Dad's carrying his racquet like a banjo
  and the bright lights from the courts
  make him look like a shiny country star.

He stops to see if Serendipity will pause.

She's following us

slipping beneath the dew-moistened bushes
raising the smell of wet leaves and earth.

She thinks she's invisible
he says, grinning.
But she's not.

Her whiteness glows against the dark.
She's a fluffy ghost
on a moonlit mission.

We begin to play
pretending we don't see her.
Each twang on the racquet
makes her tail jump
as she crouches at the end of the net
waiting.

And then the ball falls into the net
and she races to it
jumps on it
throws it in the air
and flies for freedom to the other side.

We can't help laughing

at our little kitty
Serendipity

like we do so often
these days.

Acknowledgments

Many, many thanks to the following people (and cats):

my kind and patient agent, Stephen Fraser, who loved this story when it was still a picture book and he was still an editor;

my wonderful cat-loving editor, Joy Peskin, who guided me to find the story beneath the story;

my other thoughtful editor, Catherine Frank, who helped me finish the process;

my critiquers and writing buddies, especially Janet Settimo, Peggy Reiff Miller, Mary Ann Moore, Doris Holik Kelly, Peggy Archer, Tracy Burchett, Diane Sutton, Erin Harden, Kathy Higgs-Coulthard, Kirsten Klassen, Carol Brodtrick, and George Ella Lyon;

my savior, who came to give us abundant life;

my parents, Sam and Barbara Marsh, who indulged the pet cravings of their daughters;

my husband, Marc, and my sons, Brendan and Corey, who are just as tickled by cat antics as I am;

my extended family, who have shared many a cat laugh with me, especially my sister-aunt, Kathy Hatchett-Toohey;

and finally, the cats I have lived with—Thomasina, my first cat; Stinky, the original dorm kitty; Jasmine, the fluffy white cat; Princess, the ever-reigning queen; Winnie, my first grandkitty; and Max and Murray, the cornfield boys.

I love you all.